GRANDMA MOONER

LOST HER VOICE!

By John Bianchi & Frank B. Edwards

It was Sunday, and Melody and Mortimer were ready for a visit from Grandma Mooner.

"Bad news," said Mother Mooner. "Grandma has lost her voice and can't come over today."

"That's awful," cried Mortimer.

"I think we had better go find it," said Melody.

First, they went to the hockey rink. Grandma Mooner never missed the Pokeweed Pucksters weekend games. They looked under the seats. And behind the penalty box. And on top of the scoreboard. There was no voice, but Mortimer found a broken hockey stick and a puck.

"How will she read us stories?" asked Melody.

"How will she call us for lunch?" worried Mortimer.

"We had better keep looking," they both agreed.

They went to the Opera House. Grandma Mooner loved to sing the maiden's lament in *El Pigaroni*.

They looked under the stage. And behind the curtain. And on top of the balcony. There was no voice, but Melody found some broken opera glasses and a crumpled hanky.

"How will she sing us to sleep?" asked Melody.

"How will she order popcorn at the movies?" worried Mortimer.

"We had better keep looking," they both agreed.

They went to the health club. Grandma
Mooner had recently bounced her way
to the county aerobic championships.
   They looked in the lockers. And
behind the water cooler. And under the
exercise mats. There was no voice, but
Mortimer found two shoelaces and a
polka–dot headband.

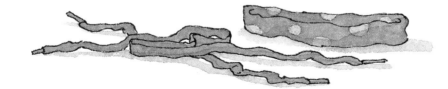

"How will she phone
us after school?"
asked Melody.

"How will she choose doughnuts for
us at the bakery?" worried Mortimer.
"We had better keep looking," they
both agreed.

They went to the wrestling arena.
Grandma Mooner had once received
autographs from both The Gruesome
Twosome Twins.

They looked under the canvas. And
behind the ticket counter. And on top
of the bell. There was no voice, but
Melody found The Red Marauder's
mask and a battered umbrella.

"How will she cheer for us at baseball?" asked Melody.

"How will she ask who wants dessert?" worried Mortimer.

"We had better keep looking," they both agreed.

"We had better go tell her we couldn't find it," said Melody.

"Maybe she left it in her refrigerator," said Mortimer hopefully.

When they arrived at Grandma Mooner's house, she was waiting for them at the front door.

"How are you, my little darlings?" she croaked softly.

"You can still talk," shouted Melody.

"You didn't lose your voice after all," sighed Mortimer.

"No, not really," laughed Grandma Mooner…

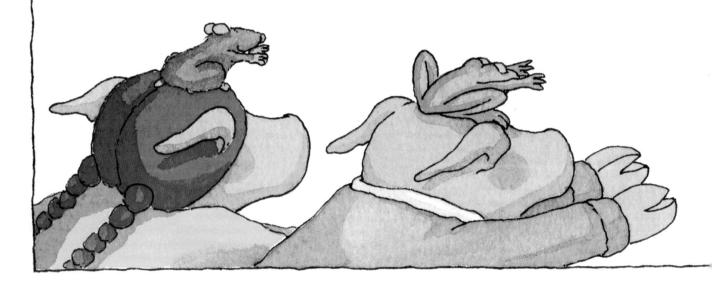